D1293780

Edited by Kate Riggs & Amy Novesky Designed by Rita Marshall
Published in 2019 by Creative Editions P.O. Box 227, Mankato, MN 56002 USA
Creative Editions is an imprint of The Creative Company www.thecreativecompany.us

Printed in China
Library of Congress Cataloging-in-Publication Data
Names: Carroll, James Christopher, author, illustrator.
Title: A song / by James Christopher Carroll.
Summary: A girl who responds to the song that calls to her serves
as an example to those who have forgotten how to listen to their lives,
how to discern music from noise, how to follow the path of
mystery and adventure set before them.
Identifiers: LCCN 2018054993 / ISBN 978-1-56846-331-5
Subjects: CYAC: Songs—Fiction. / Love—Fiction.
Classification: LCC PZ7.C2349233 Son 2019 DDC [E]—dc23
First edition 9 8 7 6 5 4 3 2 1

James Christopher Carroll

A SONG

Creative Editions

There
is a song

that calls me

through day

into dusk.

There is a song

that holds me

through dusk

into dark.

There is a song

that lifts me

through dark

into starry night.

There is a song,

a song for you.

Listen.

There is a song
that calls me

through day
into dusk.

There is a song
that holds me

through dusk
into dark.

There is a song
that lifts me

through dark
into starry night.

There is a song,
a song for you.

Listen.